P9-ANZ-289

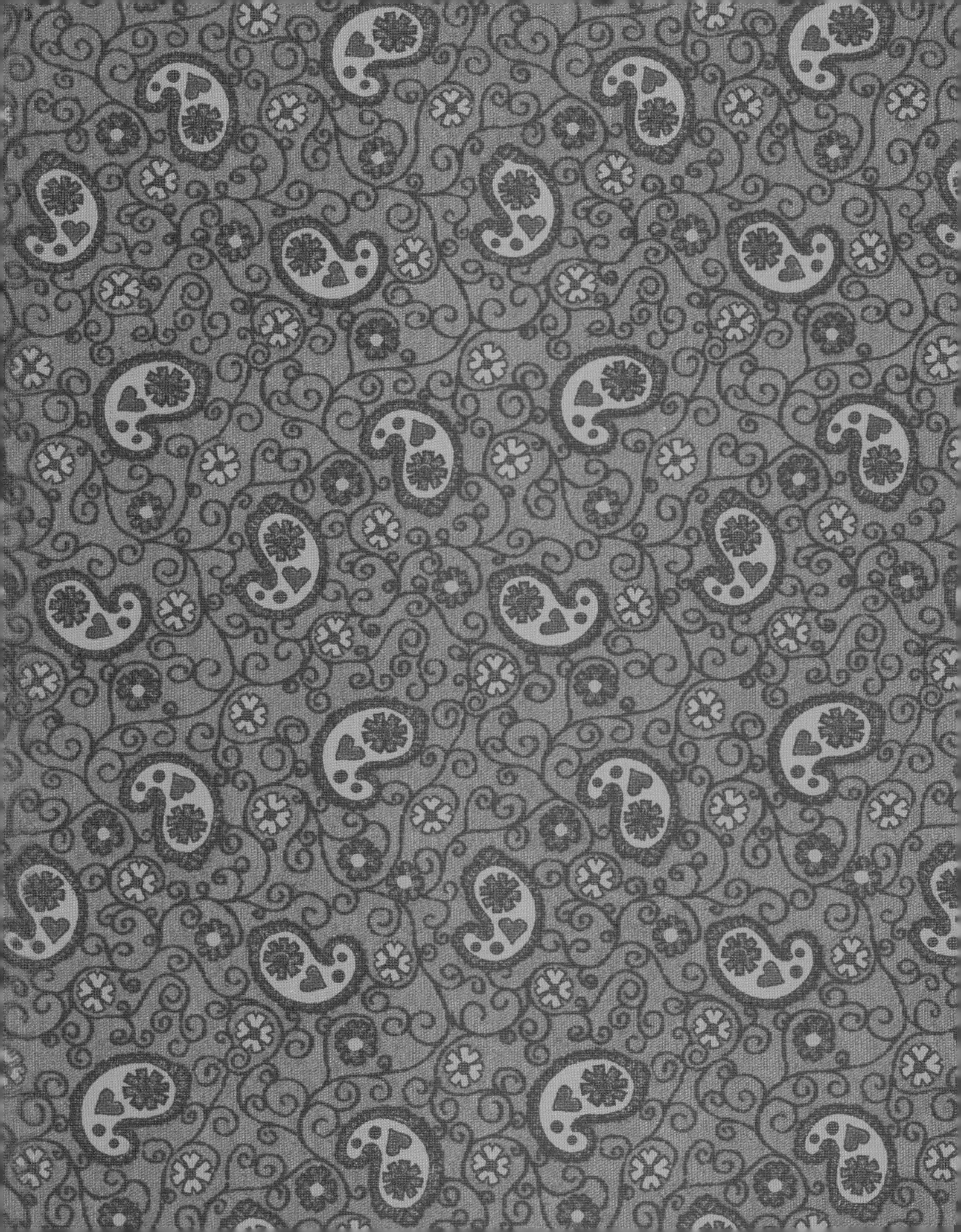

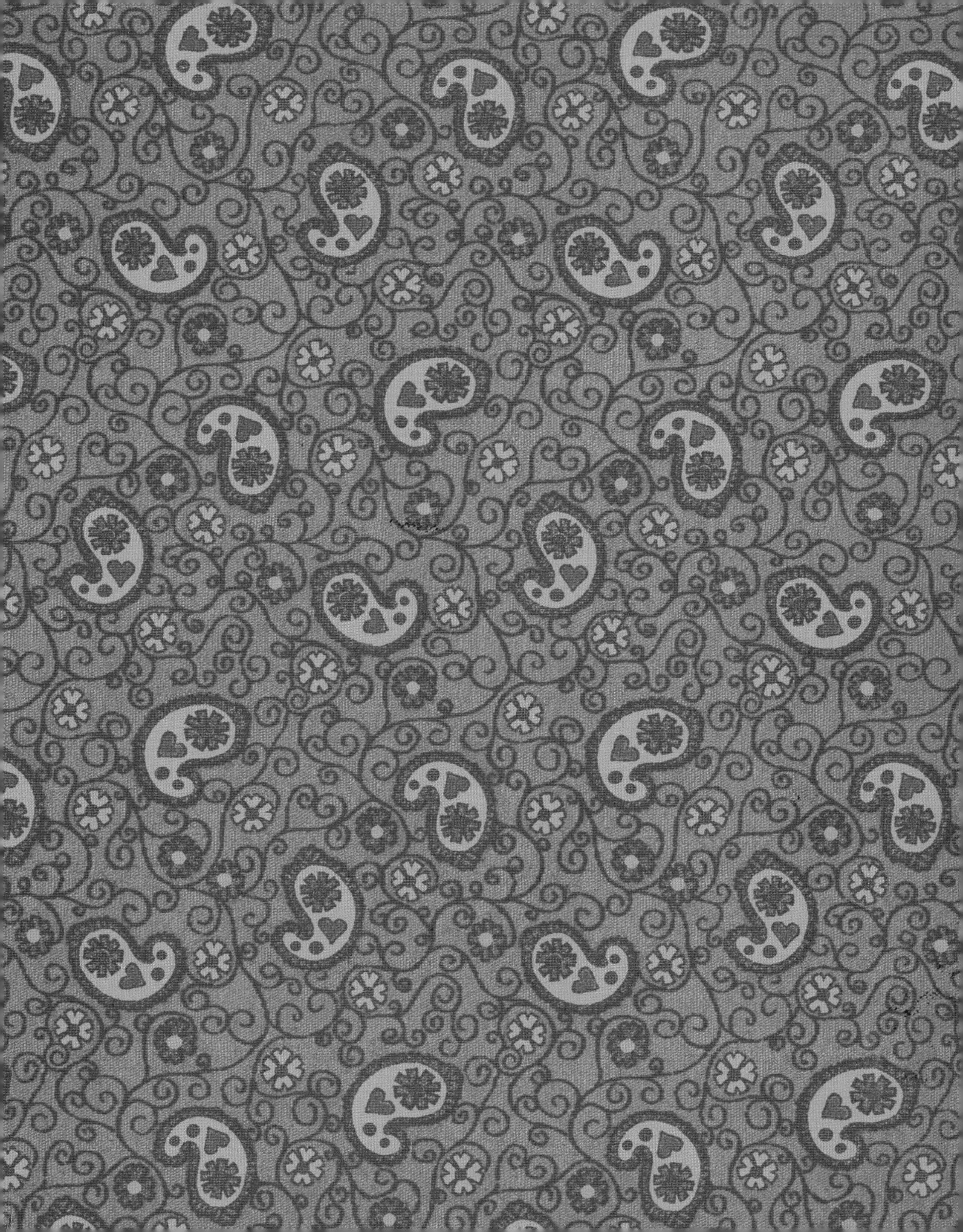

THIS IS A BORZOI BOOK PUBLISHED BY ALFRED A. KNOPF

Published in the United States of America by Alfred A. Knopf, an imprint of Random House Children's Books, a division of Random House, Inc., New York, and simultaneously in Canada by Random House of Canada Limited, Toronto.

Distributed by Random House, Inc., New York.

www.randomhouse.com/kids

Library of Congress Cataloging-in-Publication Data

Smith, Maggie, 1965–

Paisley / by Maggie Smith. — 1st ed.

p. cm.

SUMMARY: Tired of collecting dust in a toy store, a stuffed elephant named Paisley ventures out in search of his Special Someone.

ISBN 0-375-82164-3 (trade) — ISBN 0-375-92164-8 (lib. bdg.)

[1. Toys—Fiction. 2. Elephants—Fiction.] I. Title.

PZ7.S65474Pai 2004

[E]—dc22

2003024598

MANUFACTURED IN CHINA

August 2004

10 9 8 7 6 5 4 3 2 1

First Edition

Alfred A. Knopf New York

It seemed like I had been on the shelf forever.
My stuffing ached, and my ears were itchy with dust.

Day after day, the others were all finding their Perfect Match.

BIG 'n little
Toys

Toys

But nobody picked me.

Then the New Boy relocated me to foreign territory.
How would my Special Someone
ever find me there?

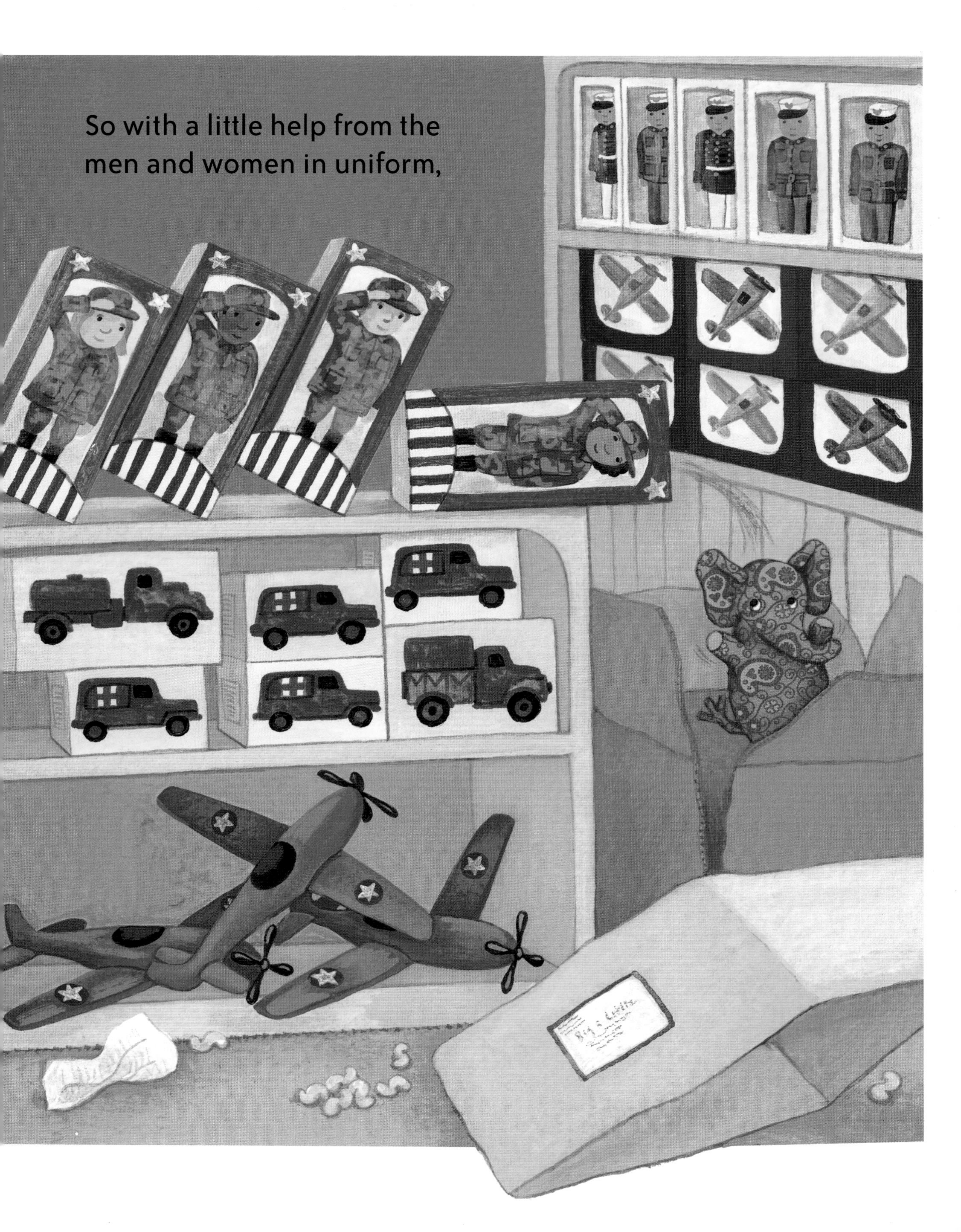

So with a little help from the
men and women in uniform,

I set out on the quest myself.

Bravely, I scouted the neighborhood, searching the faces of passersby.

I was not afraid.

I left no box unturned.

I endured rough handling,

ferocious beasts,

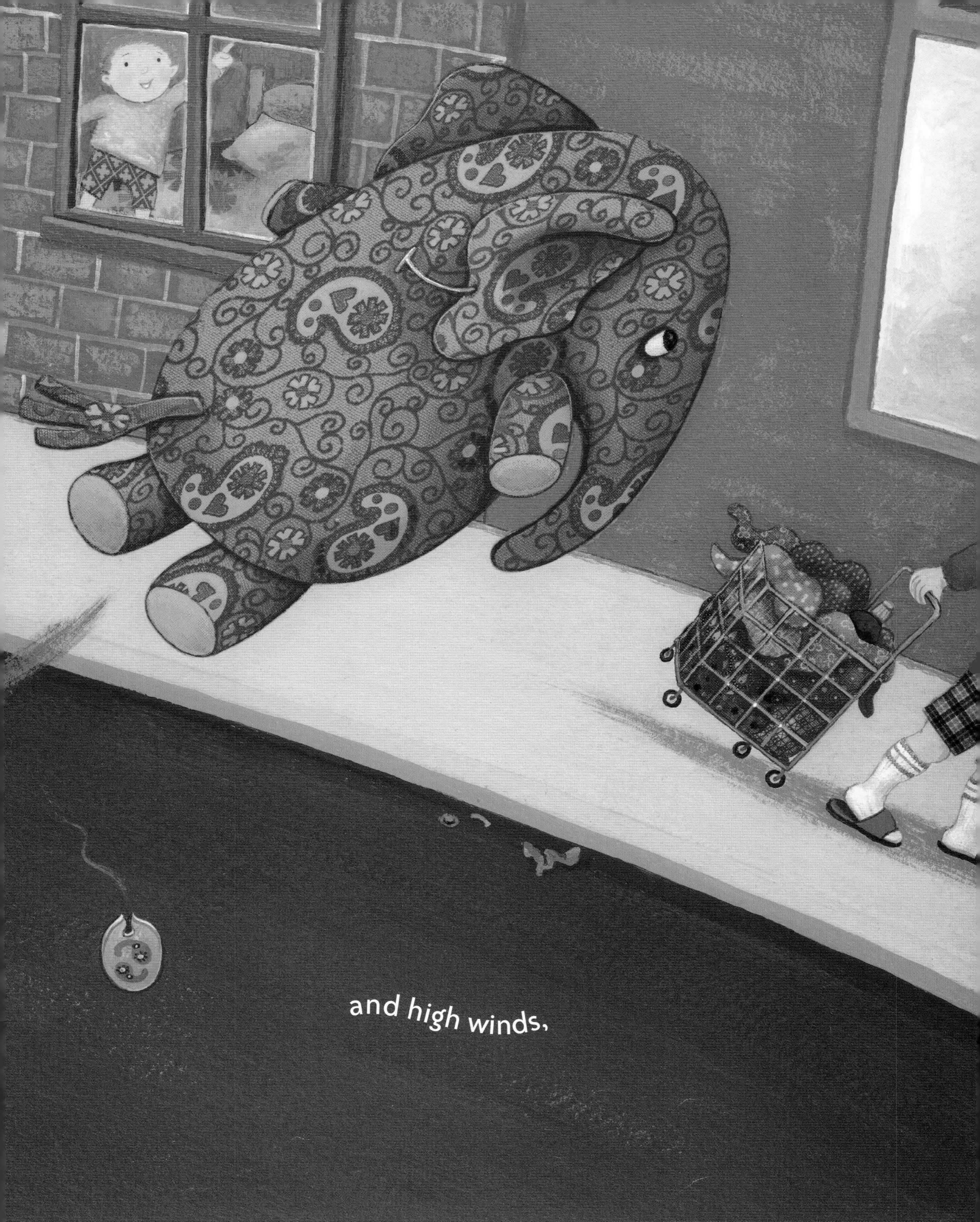

and high winds,

LOLLY'S LAU
PUSH

all in the search for my Special Someone.

I wanted to look and smell my best when we finally met, so I decided to take a bath.

Then I needed to towel off.

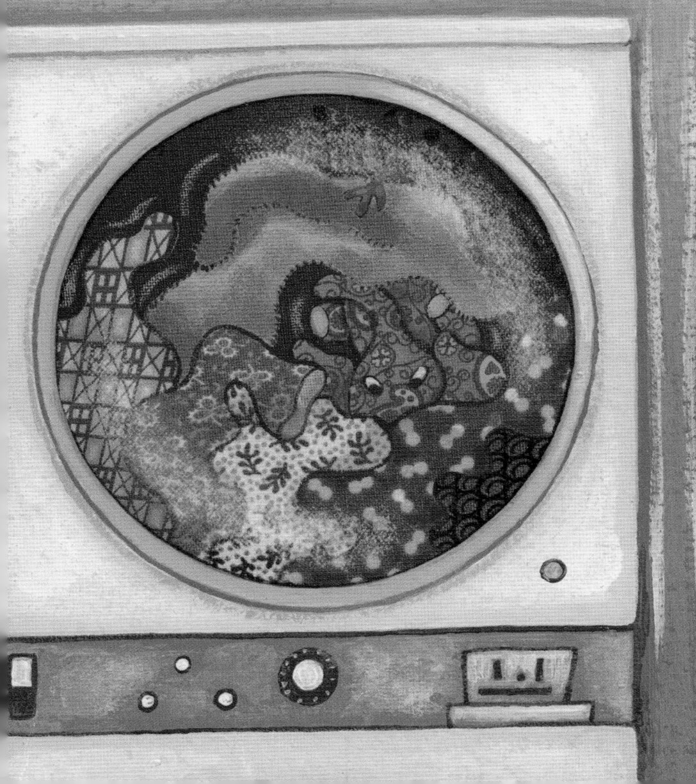

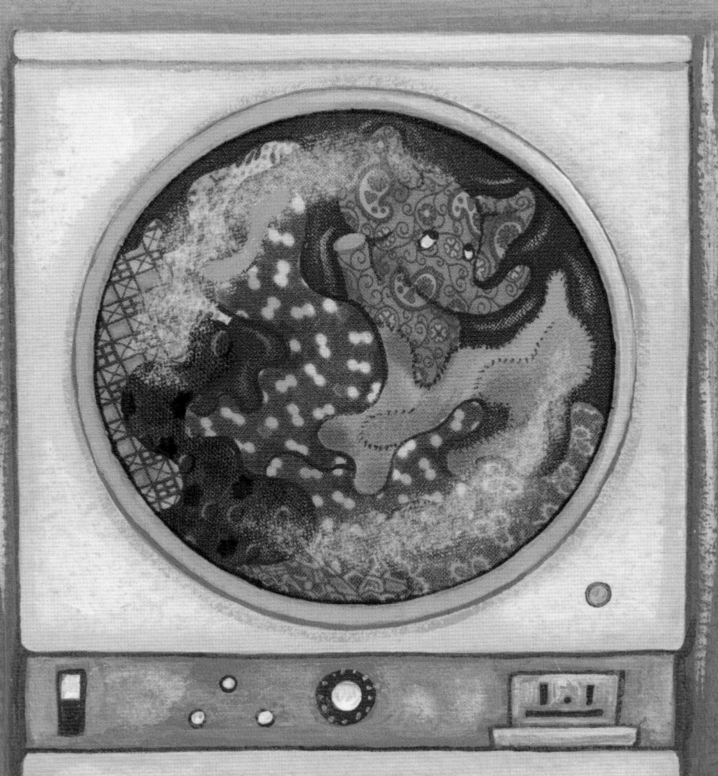

Refreshed, and feeling like a brand-new elephant,

I was ready to continue the search.

I hopped the Express to the east end of town.

But my Perfect Match did not live there.

I was back on the shelf again, a little disoriented,
but I was not discouraged. It was only a matter of time.

Looking for clues seemed like a good idea.

I looked,

and looked,

and looked.

Then the earth shook.

I could sense the presence of greatness.

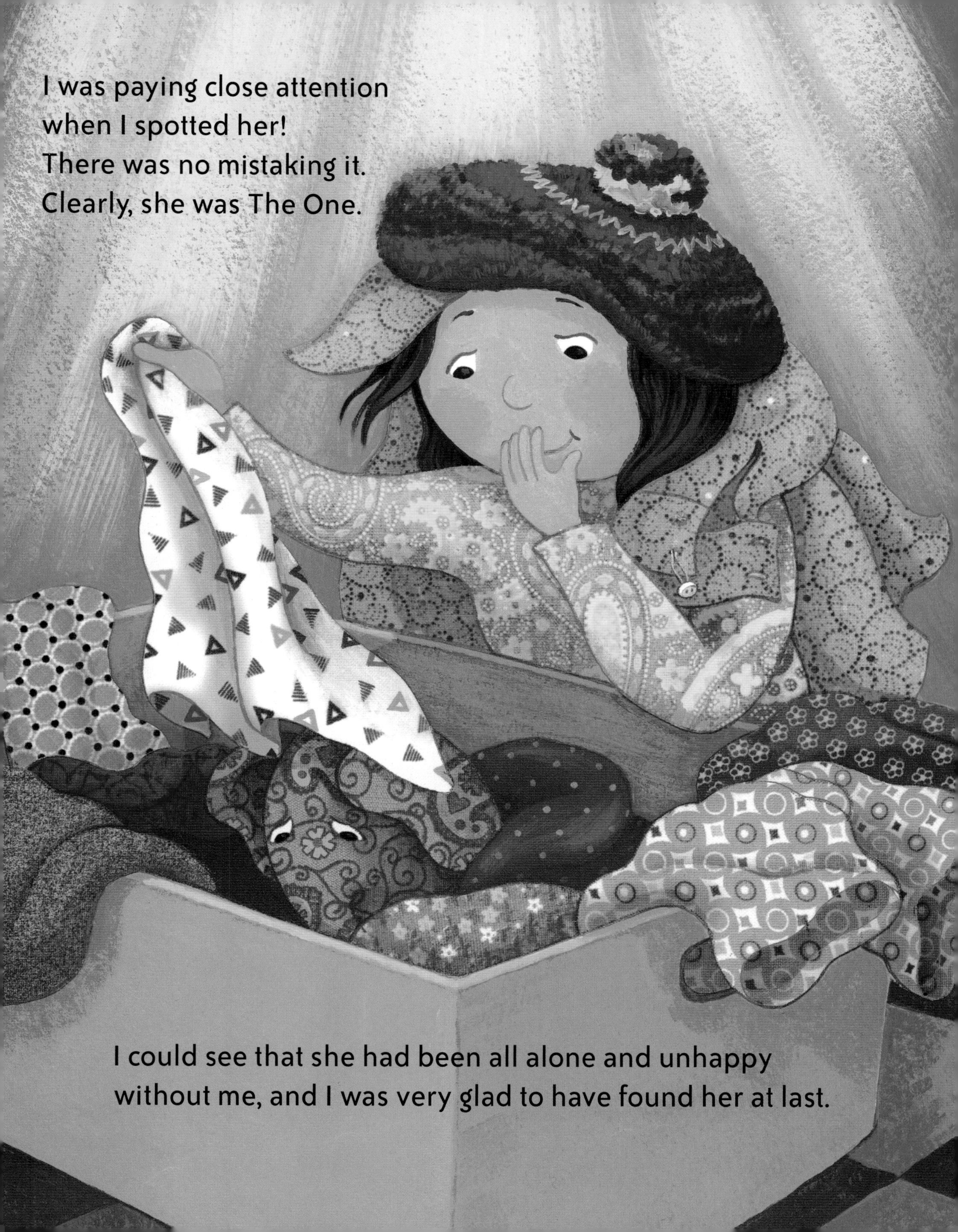

I was paying close attention
when I spotted her!
There was no mistaking it.
Clearly, she was The One.

I could see that she had been all alone and unhappy
without me, and I was very glad to have found her at last.

The Mother told her my name.
"Well, hello, Paisley," said
my little girl. "I'm Pearl!"

Then I gave her a giant hug and told her she would never be lonely again.

As we passed my old digs, I waved to the Two Misters.
I knew they could see I was finally where I belonged.

That night I got to sleep in a warm, cozy bed
for the very first time.

It was the end of a lengthy and perilous quest.
But it was only the beginning for my Perfect Match—
my Only One—my Special Pearl—and me.

Oh, an *elephant needs to be loved*, tra-la.

And a *little girl needs the right* elephant.

We're a match *made in Heaven* above, tra-la.

Finding Pearl *was like winning* a treasure hunt.

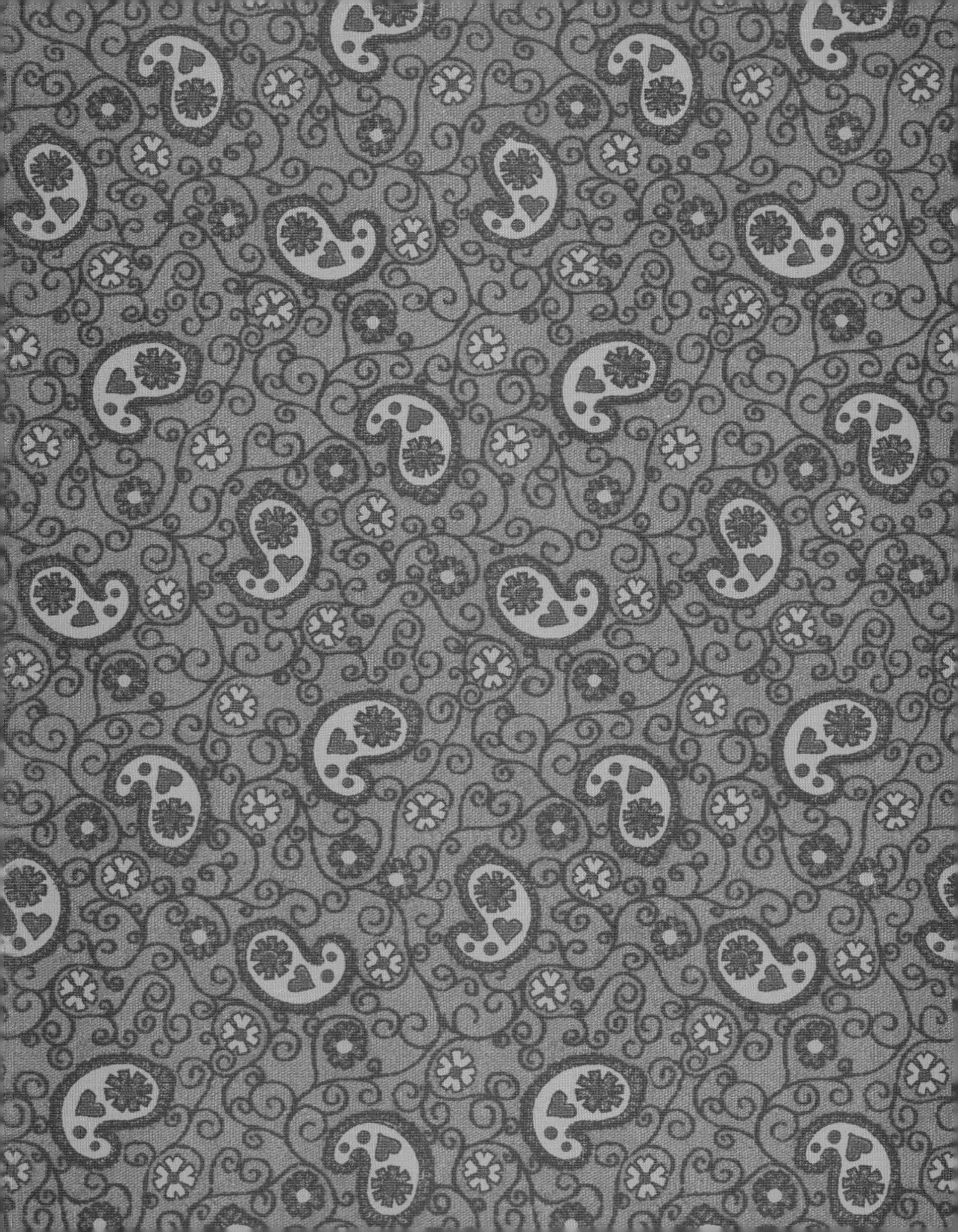

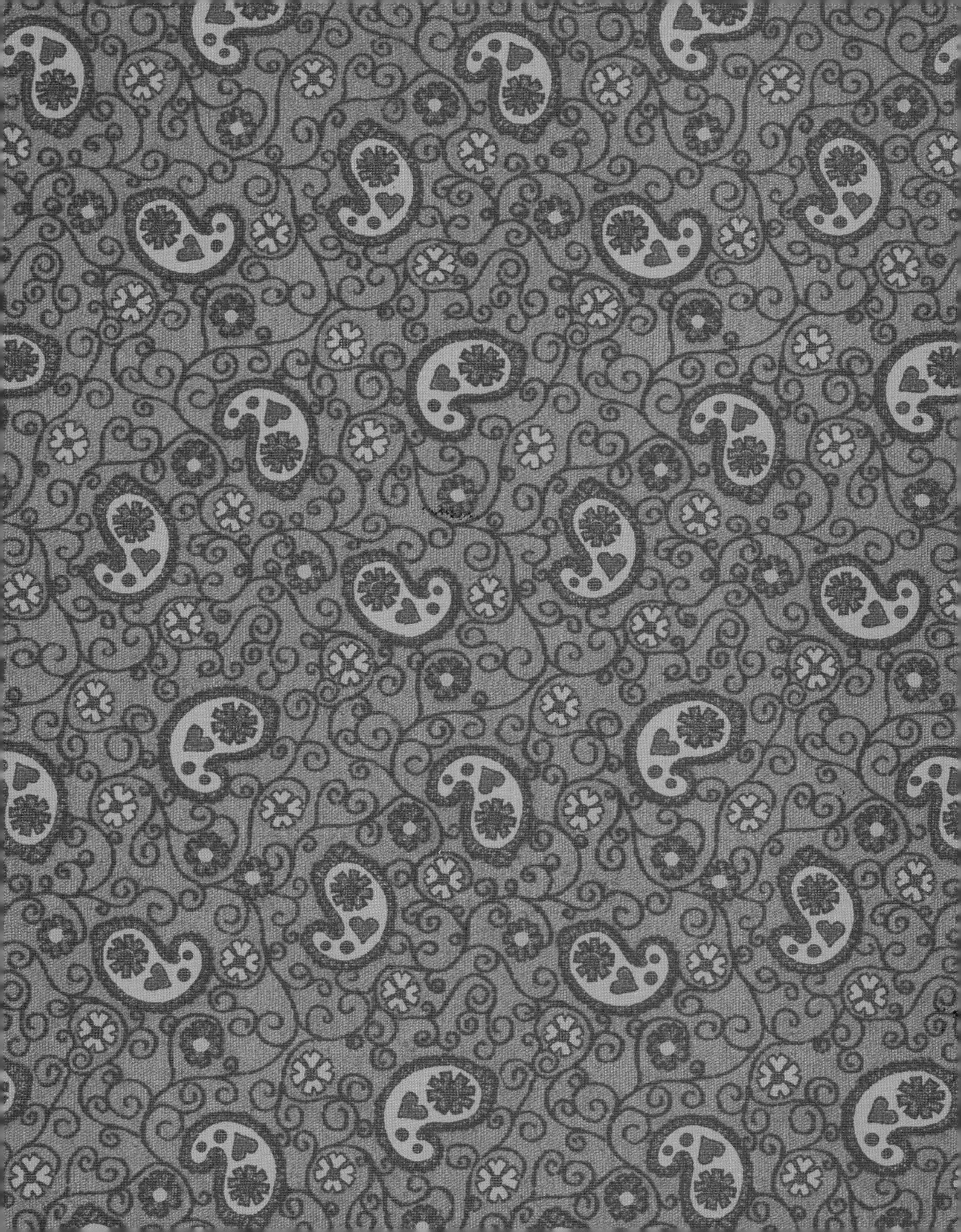